do you like t

CW00517177

LITTLE LIBRARY NUMBER TWO

BRIAN BORU

JOHN & FATTI BURKE

GILL BOOKS

Brian and his brothers and sisters grew up beside the River Shannon, near Killaloe in County Clare. Their father, Cennétig, was chieftain of the Dál gCais clan and King of Thomond.

The Vikings lived in nearby Limerick with their leader Ivar. Brian wanted to be a soldier like his father and protect his kingdom from the Viking Norsemen.

When Brian was twelve years old, his village was raided by Vikings and Brian's parents were killed. Brian's older brother Mahon became the leader of the clan. The two brothers went into the hills and forests and fought the Vikings whenever they could.

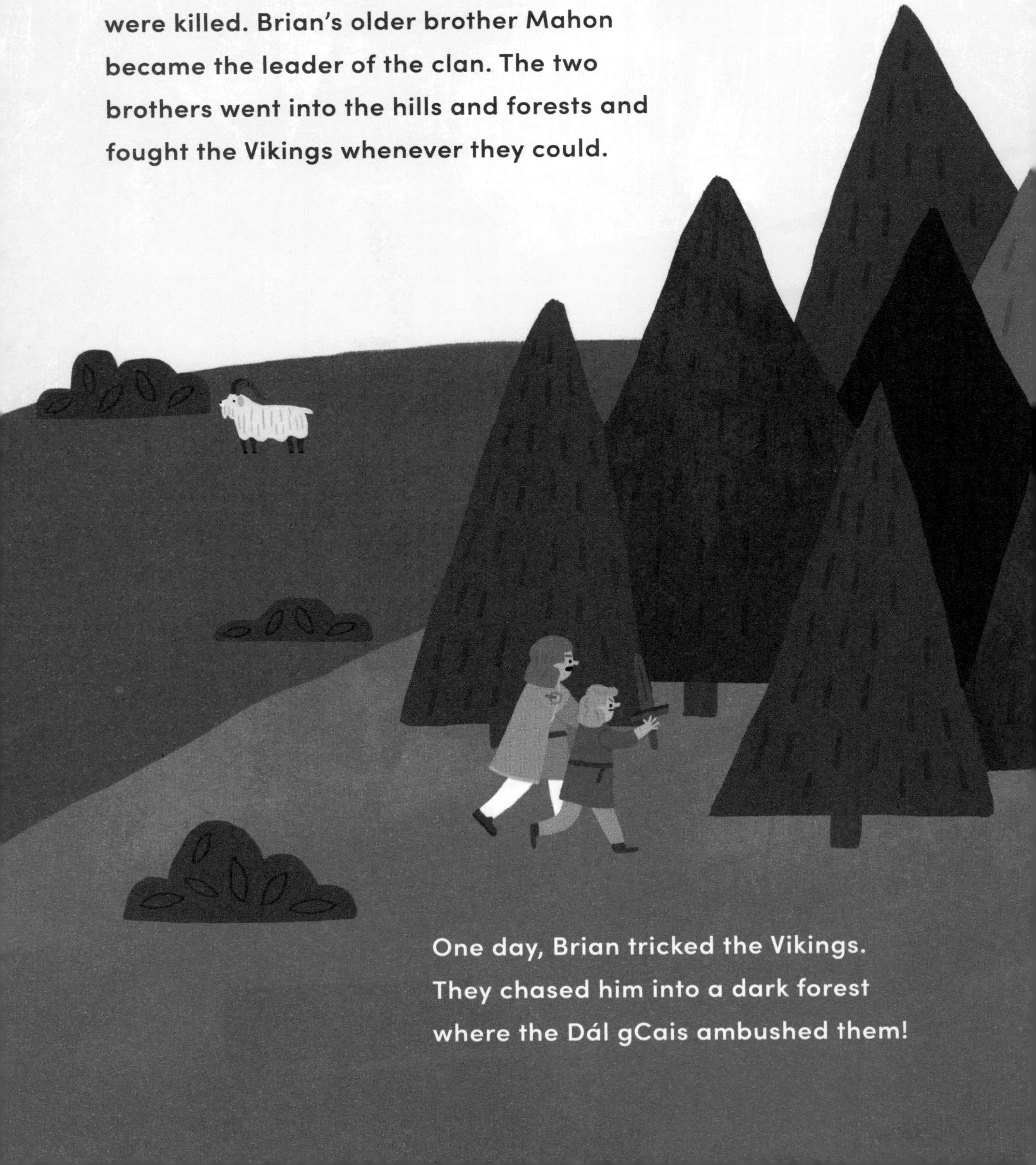

One day, Brian tricked the Vikings. They chased him into a dark forest where the Dál gCais ambushed them!

The brothers grew to be so powerful that
Mahon became King of Munster.

Years later, Mahon was murdered by one of Ivar's Viking friends. Brian was so angry that he went looking for Ivar. He chased him to Scattery Island and killed him.

Brian then captured Limerick and took control of
the Viking town of Waterford. Now Brian was King of
Munster as well as chieftain of the Dál gCais, and he
decided to make peace with the Vikings.

Meanwhile, the High King of Ireland, Malachy, had also defeated a Viking army at the Battle of Tara.

Brian went to meet the High King and they agreed to defend Ireland together.

Malachy took care of the north and Brian took care of the south.

King Malachy was at war with Máel Mórda,
the King of Leinster, and Sitric Silkenbeard,
the Viking leader of Dublin.

Brian and his son Murrough helped Malachy
to defeat the Leinster army at the Battle of
Gleann Máma.

After the battle, Máel Mórda escaped,
but was spotted hiding in a yew tree! Brian
punished him but decided to let him go.

Brian had a stronger army than Malachy, so it was agreed that Brian would become High King, also known as the Ard Rí.

Brian Boru was a good king. He repaired ruined churches and built new ones. He even replaced lost books and stolen treasures. To help pay for the work, he taxed the Vikings and Irish chieftains.

Brian loved music and poetry, so he supported harpers and singers. Brian was a fine harp player and that is why the harp is a symbol of Ireland.

Brian marched around Ireland with his army and was very popular with the people.

After many years of peace, Brian invited Máel Mórda to his palace in Clare. Máel Mórda gave some advice to Brian's sons, who were playing a game of chess. He was told to mind his own business and climb back up his yew tree!

After that insult, Máel Mórda stormed out in a temper.

As soon as Máel Mórda got back to Dublin, he and Sitric prepared for battle. Malachy heard about this and warned Brian, who gathered a huge army that included Vikings from Waterford and Limerick.

Now Máel Mórda and Sitric needed help, so they sent for more Vikings from Scotland, Orkney and the Isle of Man.

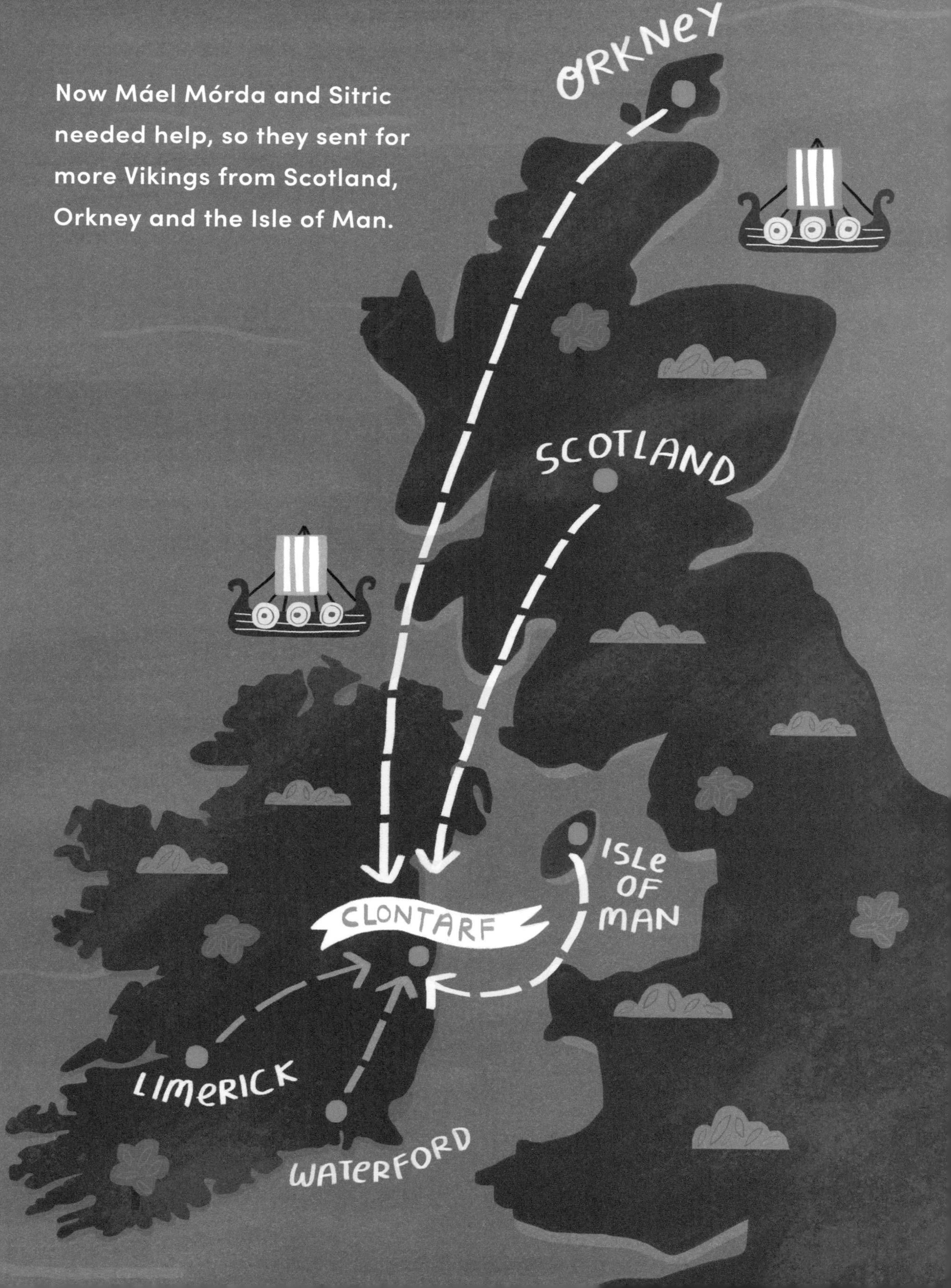
ORKNEY
SCOTLAND
ISLE OF MAN
CLONTARF
LIMERICK
WATERFORD

In April 1014 a large fleet of Viking ships arrived in Dublin Bay. But Brian and Malachy were ready for them! The two armies met in a fierce and bloody battle at Clontarf on Good Friday.

Sitric's army soon got tired and tried to retreat, but Malachy's men stopped them! Brian and Malachy's soldiers defeated the Viking and Leinster armies at the Battle of Clontarf. It was a great victory.

King Brian was too old to fight in the battle, but his son Murrough fought and was killed. Now Brian had lost his parents, his brother and his son to the Vikings.

While Brian was in his tent praying for his son,
a Viking called Brodir spotted the king, snuck
into the tent and killed him!

Everyone was very sad about Brian's death. His body was taken to Armagh, where he lies buried.

The power of the Vikings was broken and the country remained at peace for over a hundred years. Brian Boru would be remembered in Irish history for ever.

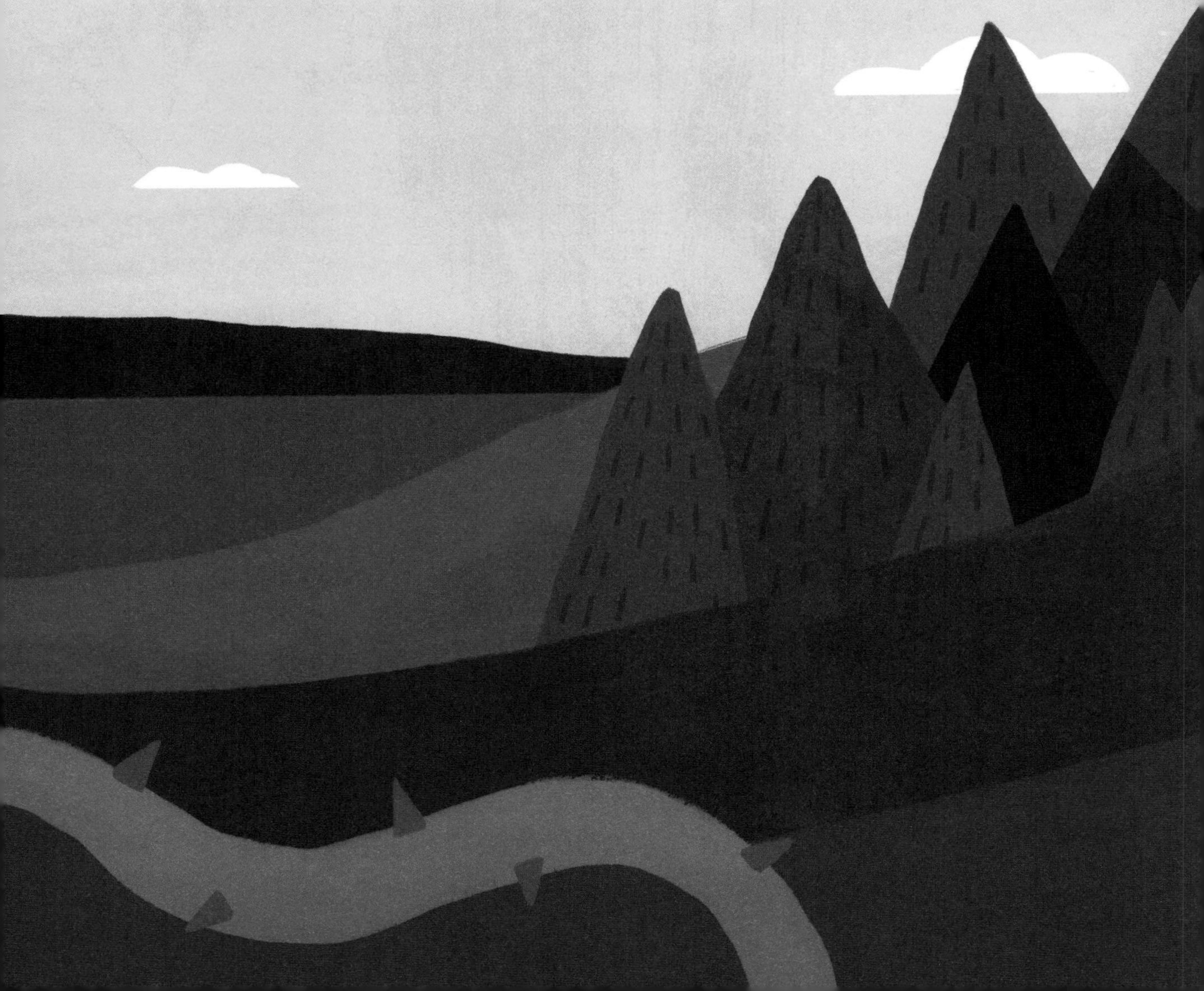

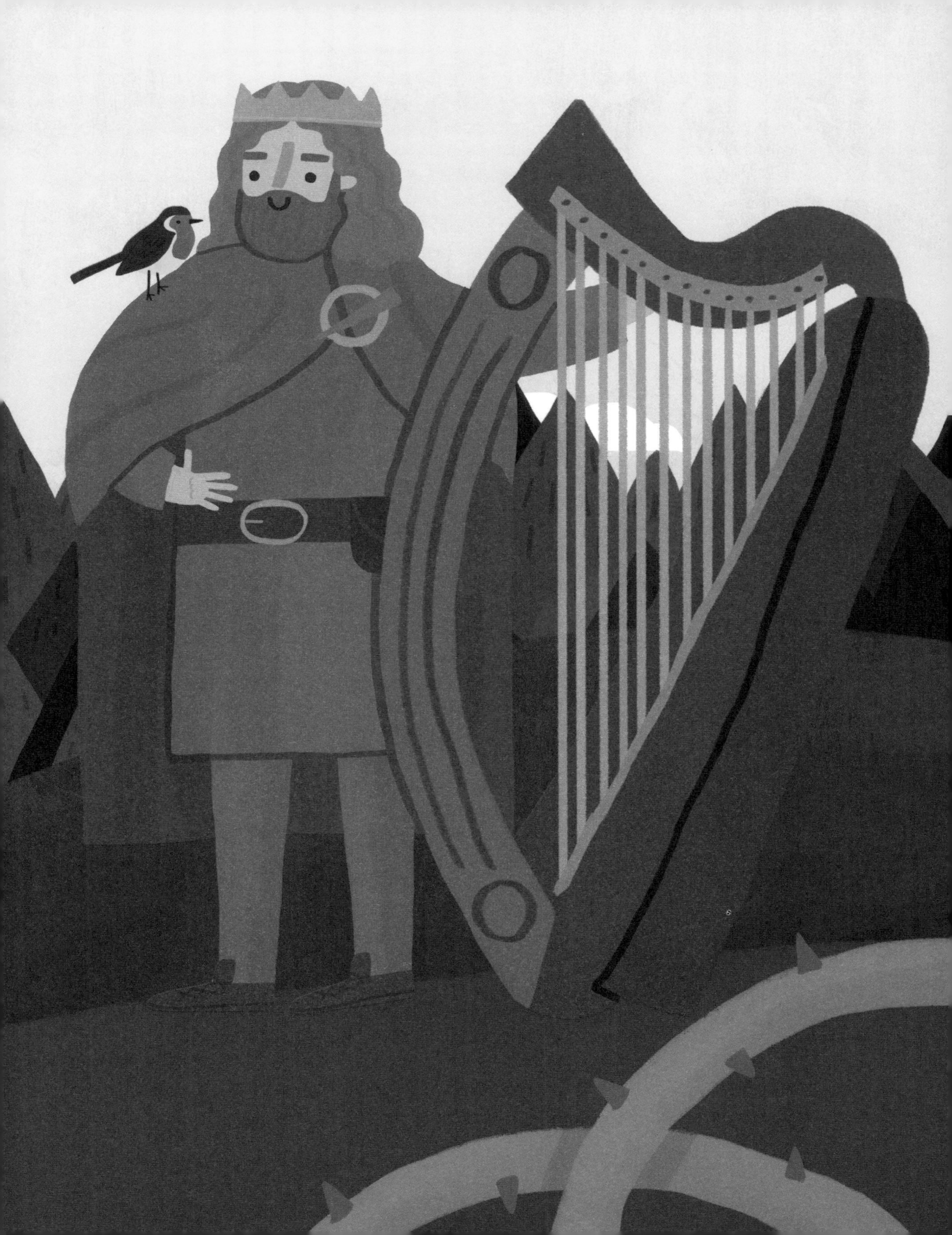

Timeline

795
Vikings arrive
in Ireland

940
Brian is born in
Kincora near Killaloe

952
Brian's parents are
killed by Vikings

964
Mahon becomes
King of Munster

977
Brian kills Ivar and makes
peace with the Vikings of
Limerick and Waterford

976
Mahon is murdered
and Brian becomes
King of Munster

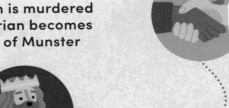

999
Máel Mórda hides in
a yew tree at the Battle
of Gleann Máma

1002
Brian becomes High
King of Ireland

997
Brian makes peace
with King Malachy

1012
Rebellion in Leinster

980
King Malachy defeats
the Dublin Vikings
at the Battle of Tara

1014
Brian dies after the
Battle of Clontarf

Did You Know?

The Brian Boru HARP in Trinity College Dublin is one of the oldest harps in the world. It is the kind of harp that Brian would have used. It is the harp that appears on IRISH COINS, PASSPORTS, GOVERNMENT LETTERS and the president's BLUE FLAG.

The NORSEMEN wore some CHAINMAIL and other ARMOUR in battle. The Irish wore LINEN TUNICS. A favourite weapon for the Irish in close combat was the IRISH BATTLE AXE.

Brian Boru's HEADQUARTERS were at KINCORA near KILLALOE. There is a Brian Boru festival in Killaloe and Ballina every year. There is also a Brian Boru Heritage Centre in Killaloe.

Brian's NAME was really BRIAN MAC CENNÉTIG. He earned the name Brian Boru (Brian of the Tributes) by collecting taxes from the lesser kings to restore the monasteries and libraries that had been destroyed.

'Brian Boru's March' is a traditional IRISH TUNE.

The name O'BRIEN was given to the families that descended from Brian Boru. The name KENNEDY comes from Brian's father, CENNÉTIG. The McMahon name also comes from the same family.

The BRIAN BORU CLUB in Wigan is one of the oldest Irish Clubs in Britain. There are camogie, GAA, fencing and handball clubs called after Brian Boru.

The most famous woman of this period of Irish history is GORMFLAITH. She was the sister of Máel Mórda. She married Olaf, the elderly Viking ruler of Dublin, and had a son called Sitric. After the Battle of Gleann Máma, Sitric Silkenbeard married Brian's daughter Sláine. With Olaf now dead, Gormflaith went on to MARRY Brian Boru! Gormflaith and Brian had a son called Donnchad. So, at the Battle of Clontarf, Gormflaith's brother and son were on one side and her husband was on the other! She and Sitric survived, but her husband, Brian, and brother, Máel Mórda, died.

ABOUT the AUTHORS

KATHI 'FATTI' BURKE is an Irish illustrator. She lives in Amsterdam.

JOHN BURKE is Fatti's dad. He is a retired primary school teacher and principal. He lives in Waterford.

Their first book, *Irelandopedia*, won *The Ryan Tubridy Show* Listeners' Choice Award at the Irish Book Awards 2015, and the Eilís Dillon Award for first children's book and the Judges' Special Award at the CBI Book of the Year Awards 2016. Their next books, *Historopedia* and *Foclóiropedia,* were nominated for the Specsavers Children's Book of the Year (Junior) Award at the Irish Book Awards 2016 and 2017. Their books have sold over 100,000 copies in Ireland.

ALSO in the LITTLE LIBRARY SERIES

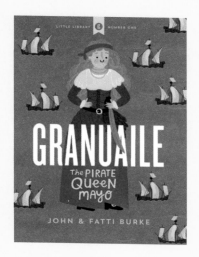

BOOK ONE

ALSO by the AUTHORS

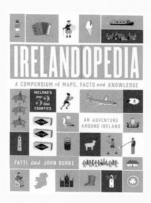

Gill Books

Hume Avenue

Park West

Dublin 12

www.gillbooks.ie

Gill Books is an imprint of M.H. Gill and Co.

Text © John Burke 2019
Illustrations © Kathi Burke 2019
978 07171 8456 9

Designed by www.grahamthew.com
Printed by L&C Group, Poland
This book is typeset in 13pt on 25pt Sofia Pro.

The paper used in this book comes from the wood pulp of
managed forests. For every tree felled, at least one tree is
planted, thereby renewing natural resources.

All rights reserved.
No part of this publication may be copied, reproduced or
transmitted in any form or by any means, without written
permission of the publishers.

A CIP catalogue record for this book is available
from the British Library.

5 4 3 2 1